What the Ladybird Heard at the Seaside

JULIA DONALDSON

LYDIA MONKS

M OOKS

One July, when the sun was high,
The ladybird took to the clear blue sky.
She spread her wings in the summer breeze
And flew over farms and fields and trees.
She flew and she flew, as fast as could be
Till at last she came to the deep salt sea.

And the sea lion roared and
the seagull shrieked,

The mermaid sang and
the dolphin squeaked.

The crab went SNAP and
the shark went GNASH.

The whale's grey tail made a mighty SPLASH.

The dogfish barked and the catfish purred,

But the ladybird said never a word.

But the ladybird saw, and the ladybird heard . . .

She saw two men in a camper van,
With swimming trunks and a cunning plan.
(They were Hefty Hugh and Lanky Len,
Up to their wicked ways again.)

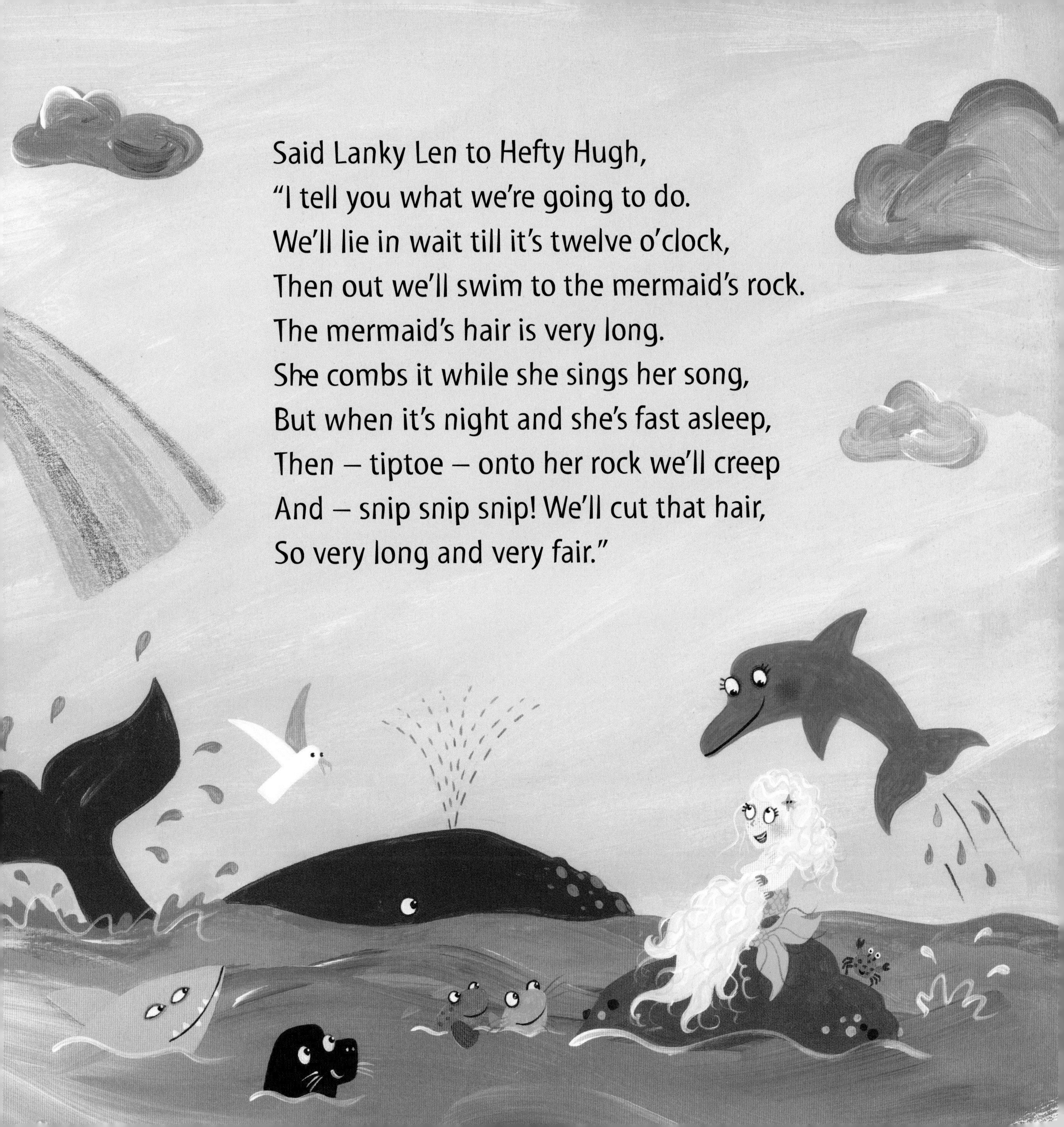

Said Lanky Len to Hefty Hugh,
"I tell you what we're going to do.
We'll lie in wait till it's twelve o'clock,
Then out we'll swim to the mermaid's rock.
The mermaid's hair is very long.
She combs it while she sings her song,
But when it's night and she's fast asleep,
Then – tiptoe – onto her rock we'll creep
And – snip snip snip! We'll cut that hair,
So very long and very fair."

Said Hefty Hugh to Lanky Len,
"We'll make a lovely wig, and then
We'll sell it to a famous star.
What brilliant, brainy blokes we are!

The mermaid's hair will soon grow back,
Enough to fill another sack!
We'll keep on doing it forever.
We've hit on something really clever!"

The little spotty ladybird
Who hardly ever spoke a word
Told the animals what she'd heard.

Then the sea lion roared and the seagull shrieked,
The mermaid wailed and the dolphin squeaked.
The crab went SNAP and the shark went GNASH.
The whale's grey tail made a mighty SPLASH,
And the fish declared, "That wicked pair!
We can't let them steal the mermaid's hair."

But the ladybird had a good idea
And she whispered it into every ear.

Then the seagull gave a joyful shriek
And he fetched some seaweed in his beak,
And as the sky was turning red
He dropped it onto the sea lion's head.

Then as the sky was turning black
The sea lion climbed on the whale's humped back . . .

The clock struck twelve, and the two bad men,
Hefty Hugh and Lanky Len,
Flip-flapped down to the salty sea.
It was cold and dark but they laughed with glee.

Then the whale began to sing a song.
"That's her!" said Hugh. "We can't go wrong!"

They swam towards the tuneful sound.
"She's still awake," said Len, and frowned.

The singing stopped. They took a peep.
Said Hugh, "I think she's gone to sleep."

Up they climbed, with their big brown sack,
Onto the whale's enormous back,
And – snip snip snip – they started snipping.
"This hair," said Hugh, "is damp and dripping."

"What's more," said Len, "it's awfully tough.
Our scissors can't be sharp enough."

Then, "Help!" cried Hugh. "This rock is heaving.
I think we'd better both be leaving."
But Len replied, "Just one more snip!"

Then the whale's grey tail gave a great big FLIP.

The thieves fell into the water – SPLOSH!
And Hugh said, "Golly!" and Len said, "Gosh!"

Then, “Ouch!” cried Hugh and Len yelled, “No!”
As the shark bit a flipper and the crab pinched a toe.

They swam for their lives, and then they ran
All the way back to their camper van.

“Phew!” said Hugh. “We’ve had a scare,
But at least we’ve got the mermaid’s hair.”
They opened up the sack, and then –

“It’s full of seaweed!” shouted Len,
And “Tricked again!” said the two bad men.

Then the sea lion roared and the seagull shrieked,
The mermaid sang and the dolphin squeaked.
The crab went SNAP and the shark went GNASH.
The whale's grey tail made a mighty SPLASH.
The dogfish barked and the catfish purred,

But the ladybird said never a word.

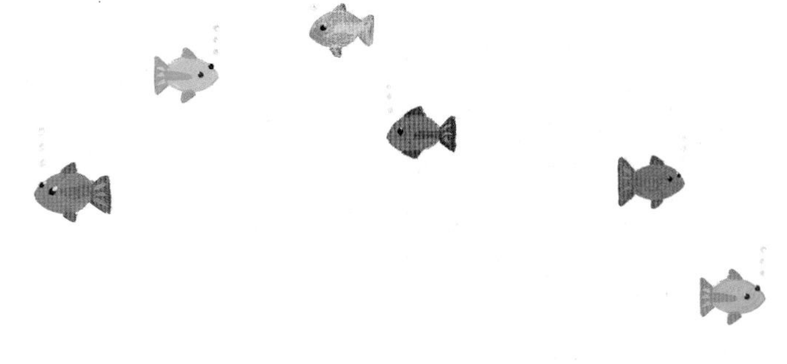

For Francesca ~ JD

For Órlagh and Fergal ~ LM

First published 2020 by Macmillan Children's Books
This edition published 2021 by Macmillan Children's Books
an imprint of Pan Macmillan
The Smithson, 6 Briset Street, London EC1M 5NR
Associated companies throughout the world.
www.panmacmillan.com

ISBN: 978-1-5290-2315-2

1 3 5 7 9 8 6 4 2

A CIP catalogue record for this book is available from the British Library.

Printed in China.